AUSTRALIAN NIGHTMARES

Terrifying Tales from Down Under

**Written and Illustrated by
Heather Mallia**

AUSTRALIAN NIGHTMARES

Australian Nightmares

Heather Mallia

CONTENTS

To Mum,
For always encouraging my stories and believing in me, no matter how spooky they get. Your love and support mean everything.

With all my love,
Heather

Author Quote

"Australia is a land of breathtaking beauty, where the sun kisses the ocean and the wilderness whispers secrets. But beneath the brilliance lies a darkness—where creatures unseen wait in the shadows, and the land itself can turn deadly with a single misstep. Here, beauty and danger are woven together, and to love it is to dance with both light and terror."

Heather Mallia

1

THE HOWL OF THE OUTBACK

In the remote outback town of Hollow Springs, Halloween was more than just a night for lollies; it was a time for ghost stories, spine-tingling legends, and the occasional chill in the air. Four friends—Timothy, Arabella, Stevie, and Grace—were excitedly gearing up for their annual Halloween adventure.

Timothy, the leader of the group, had a wild mop of curly hair and a knack for daring ideas. He wore a tattered vampire cape that flared dramatically as he moved. Arabella, with her long dark hair and thoughtful demeanour, dressed as a witch, complete with a crooked hat that always seemed to tilt just a bit too far. Stevie, the class clown, sported an oversized skeleton costume that made him look comically large. Lastly, Grace, the youngest and most adventurous, opted for a fierce pirate look, complete with a plastic sword and a fake parrot perched on her shoulder.

"Alright, mates, are we ready to hit the streets?" Timothy called, glancing around at his friends. The air was buzzing with excitement.

"Absolutely!" Grace replied, twirling her sword. "I've been waiting for this all year!"

"Let's make sure to hit Old Man Thompson's place first," Stevie suggested, his eyes gleaming. "He always gives out the good stuff!"

"Yeah, and we need to be careful not to miss the big oak tree. That's where the legend is," Arabella reminded them, her voice dropping to a whisper.

"What legend?" Grace asked, raising an eyebrow.

"The Legend of the Howling Wombat," Arabella explained, her eyes sparkling with mischief. "They say that if you're out on Halloween night and you hear its howl, it means you're in for some serious trouble. It's supposed to be a massive wombat that prowls the outback, searching for trick-or-treaters to scare away. If it catches you... well, let's just say it likes to keep its sweets to itself."

"Sounds like a load of bull!" Stevie laughed. "What's a wombat gonna do? Steal my lollies? Please!"

"Don't be so sure, mate," Timothy said, his tone half-serious. "I reckon we might just run into it tonight."

With that, they set off into the moonlit streets, the soft crunch of leaves underfoot accompanying their chatter.

As they approached Old Man Thompson's house, they were greeted by flickering jack-o'-lanterns and the sound of eerie music drifting through the air.

"Oi, Thompson!" Timothy called as they approached the old man's porch. "Got any treats for us?"

"Only the best for the brave, eh?" Thompson chuckled, tossing handfuls of candy into their bags. "Just watch yourselves out there. You never know what you might encounter on a night like this!"

"Thanks, mate!" Grace beamed, her eyes shining with the thrill of the night.

As they moved from house to house, the town seemed to come alive. Shadows danced in the corners of their vision, and strange sounds echoed through the stillness. They shared ghost stories, laughing and teasing each other as they walked.

Suddenly, as they approached the large oak tree at the centre of town, the atmosphere shifted. A low rumble of thunder rolled overhead, and the moon was briefly hidden by clouds.

"Uh, guys? I think we should head back," Arabella said, her voice shaky. "This feels... off."

"Nah, come on! Let's just check it out," Timothy urged, grinning. "What's a bit of spookiness, right?"

As they gathered around the tree, a sharp howl cut through the air, sending chills down their spines. It echoed eerily, resonating in their bones.

"That wasn't just a dog, was it?" Stevie asked, his bravado wavering.

"No way! That was the Howling Wombat!" Grace exclaimed, her eyes wide. "What if it's really out here?"

"Let's not stick around to find out," Arabella said, her voice barely above a whisper.

But Timothy, emboldened by the thrill, raised his voice. "Come on! We've got to see what it is!"

Just then, a shadow moved between the trees, and they could see glowing eyes peering out from the darkness. The howl sounded again, closer this time.

"Timothy, let's go!" Arabella cried, grabbing his arm.

But he shook her off, stepping closer to the ominous shadow. "No, wait! What if it's just a myth? We need to find out!"

Before anyone could stop him, he shouted, "Show yourself!"

In an instant, the figure lunged forward—a massive wombat, larger than any they had seen before, with sharp teeth and glowing eyes that pierced the darkness. It stood on its hind legs, growling fiercely.

"Run!" Grace screamed, drawing her plastic sword as they all turned to flee.

They sprinted down the street, adrenaline pumping. The sound of the creature's claws scraping against the ground echoed behind them.

"Where do we go?" Stevie yelled, panicked. "It's right behind us!"

"Into the bush! We can lose it in the trees!" Timothy shouted, leading the way as they dashed into the thick underbrush, trying to navigate the unfamiliar terrain.

The howling grew louder, almost mocking them, as they stumbled deeper into the darkness. The trees loomed overhead, twisting and turning, their branches resembling skeletal fingers reaching out to grab them.

"Timothy, this was a terrible idea!" Arabella panted, glancing back over her shoulder.

"Yeah, mate, you really stuffed this one up!" Stevie added, struggling to keep pace.

Grace brandished her sword, her voice shaking but defiant. "I won't let it take our candy! We have to fight!"

As they stopped to catch their breath, the howling ceased, replaced by an eerie silence. They huddled together, glancing around nervously.

"What do we do now?" Timothy asked, his bravado fading.

"I—I don't know," Arabella admitted, fear creeping into her voice. "But we can't just stay here."

Suddenly, the glowing eyes appeared again, this time closer. The wombat emerged from the shadows, its growl vibrating through the air.

"Back away!" Timothy shouted, but the creature was too fast. It lunged at them, and they scrambled to escape.

In the chaos, they stumbled into a clearing, where the moonlight illuminated the ground. They could see footprints—huge, clawed tracks leading into the thick brush.

"What if it's waiting for us to go back?" Grace whispered, her voice trembling.

"We can't just sit here!" Stevie urged. "We've got to get out of here!"

They turned to run, but as they did, the howl returned, piercing the night with a bone-chilling echo. At that moment, everything went dark. The ground trembled beneath them, and they felt an otherworldly force pulling them down.

"Timothy! Arabella! Grace!" Stevie cried, but the shadows consumed them, one by one.

And just like that, they vanished.

The next morning, Hollow Springs returned to its usual quiet. The townsfolk bustled about, oblivious to the missing teens. As Halloween faded into memory, whispers of the Howling Wombat grew louder, with tales of four friends who had dared to challenge the legend and were never seen again.

2

THE DEPTHS OF THE HAWKESBURY

In a small town nestled along the banks of the Hawkesbury River, whispers of an ancient legend danced through the air. The locals spoke in hushed tones about a monstrous creature lurking beneath the water's surface, waiting for its next unwary victim. The river, winding its way through dense bushland, held both beauty and terror—a stark reminder of nature's wild heart.

One sunny Saturday morning, old Jack Turner, a wiry man with a weathered face and a twinkle in his eye, decided to take his grandson, Toby, out fishing. Toby, a sprightly twelve-year-old with tousled hair and boundless energy, was thrilled at the prospect.

"Ready for a ripper of a day, mate?" Jack grinned, loading their gear into an old tinny boat.

"Absolutely, Grandpa! I can't wait to catch some whoppers!" Toby replied, bouncing on his toes.

As they pushed off into the gentle waters, the sun glimmered on the river's surface. The only sounds were the soft lapping of waves and the calls of distant cockatoos. Jack steered the boat upstream, navigating familiar bends.

"Now, Toby, before we get too comfy, I've gotta tell ya 'bout a little story," Jack said, his voice dropping to a conspiratorial whisper.

Toby leaned in, intrigued. "What is it?"

"Ever heard of the Hawkesbury Monster?" Jack asked, his eyes narrowing dramatically.

Toby shook his head. "Nah, but it sounds epic!"

Jack chuckled, casting his line into the water. "Well, legend has it that a massive creature lurks in these waters. They say it's got scales as thick as a croc's and a mouth big enough to swallow a whole goat."

"Seriously?!" Toby's eyes went wide. "What does it look like?"

"They reckon it's like a giant eel crossed with a barramundi," Jack explained, reeling in his line slightly. "But it's no ordinary fish. It's smart and sneaky, waiting for folks to swim or fish out here before it strikes."

"Do you really think it exists?" Toby asked, glancing nervously at the dark water.

"Who knows?" Jack shrugged, feigning nonchalance. "But I wouldn't go swimming in this river after hearing the stories. Best stick to fishing, eh?"

Toby shivered, glancing at the water. "Maybe we should just fish and not think about it."

As they cast their lines, Jack recounted tales of locals who had gone missing after fishing trips, their boats found drifting and empty. Each story added to the suspense, leaving Toby both thrilled and frightened.

"Grandpa, do you think it's true? Like, what if it comes after us?" Toby asked, trying to mask his apprehension with bravado.

"Ah, don't worry, mate," Jack chuckled, flicking his line again. "It's just an old yarn to keep the kids outta the water. Now, let's see if we can hook something decent."

Hours passed, and the sun dipped lower in the sky. They hadn't caught much, just a couple of small bream. As the light began to fade, Jack decided it was time to head back.

"Alright, Toby. Let's pack it in before it gets too dark. You know the old saying: 'the river holds secrets when the sun goes down,'" he said with a grin.

As they turned the boat around, the river began to grow eerily quiet, the only sound being the gentle splash of oars against the water. But then, a low rumble echoed beneath them, causing Jack to stop paddling.

"What was that?" Toby asked, his voice trembling.

"Probably just a log shifting in the current," Jack replied, but the unease crept into his voice.

Suddenly, the water erupted with a tremendous splash, sending waves crashing against the boat. Both of them scrambled to keep their balance.

"What the—?" Jack exclaimed, eyes wide.

From the depths, a massive figure surged upwards, scales glinting in the fading light. It was the Hawkesbury Monster, a nightmarish creature with a long, sinuous body and enormous, glaring eyes. Its gaping mouth opened, revealing rows of sharp teeth that glistened like daggers.

"Grandpa!" Toby screamed, panic surging through him. "What do we do?!"

"Row! Row like you've never rowed before!" Jack yelled, his hands gripping the oars with a desperate strength.

As they frantically paddled away, the creature dove beneath the surface, creating waves that rocked their tiny boat. Jack's heart raced, and he felt an overwhelming need to protect his grandson.

But the monster was relentless, surfacing beside them, its huge eye watching them intently. With a sudden, powerful thrust, it lunged at the boat, sending them both sprawling into the cold water.

Toby gasped as the frigid river enveloped him. He surfaced, sputtering, and looked around for Jack. The old man had managed to hold onto the side of the boat, but the monster was circling, its massive body gliding effortlessly through the water.

"Grandpa!" Toby cried, panic rising in his chest. "We need to get out of here!"

"Climb back in!" Jack shouted, struggling to keep the boat steady. "Don't let it get you!"

As Toby reached for the edge, the creature lunged again, water spraying everywhere. Jack felt a surge of fear. They had to escape—fast.

With one final effort, he pulled himself into the boat, but the monster's shadow loomed closer. They could see its jagged teeth glinting in the last rays of sunlight.

"Get the oars, Toby! We have to paddle!" Jack yelled, his voice strained.

But just then, the monster rose from the depths, its massive head looming over the boat, the air thick with an unnatural chill. In a flash, it snapped its jaws, and the world went dark.

As the water settled and the echoes of terror faded, Jack Turner and Toby awoke on the riverbank, gasping for air. They were soaked, their hearts pounding as the memory of the monstrous creature loomed large in their minds.

"Toby! Are you alright?" Jack gasped, shaking the water from his hair as he scrambled to his feet.

"I think so, Grandpa," Toby replied, trembling as he looked at his grandfather. "What just happened?"

"We barely made it out," Jack said, his voice low and urgent. "That thing... it nearly had us. We need to warn the others."

They quickly made their way back to town, the sun rising over the horizon and casting a golden light over the familiar landscape. But instead of relief, an unsettling weight hung in the air. The two arrived at the local pub, where a few early risers were gathered for breakfast.

"Jack! Toby!" called out old Bert, a grizzled fisherman with a weathered face. "You boys look like you've seen a ghost!"

"Worse, Bert!" Jack exclaimed, rushing into the pub. "We encountered the Hawkesbury Monster! It's real, and it's dangerous!"

The patrons exchanged sceptical glances, but Jack pressed on. "We were fishing, and it attacked us! We barely got away. You have to keep your kids out of the water, especially after dark!"

Toby nodded, his eyes wide. "I swear, it's not just a story! It's waiting for anyone who dares to swim or sail here!"

Instead of fear, a wave of laughter erupted from the group. "Oh, come on, Jack! You're telling tall tales again!" one man chuckled, clapping Jack on the back.

"Yeah, kids have been swimming in that river for years! It's just an old wives' tale!" Bert scoffed.

Frustration welled within Jack as he glanced at Toby, who looked crestfallen. "I'm serious! We almost lost everything!"

But the laughter continued, and soon Jack and Toby left the pub, disheartened. They knew the truth, yet no one would listen. As they walked home, the weight of their encounter hung heavy in the air.

Days turned into weeks, and the chilling memory began to fade, but not for Toby. He couldn't shake the feeling that someone might challenge the legend. Just as he feared, whispers started circulating among his friends.

One evening, gathered around a campfire, Toby overheard his mates, Sam and Ben, teasing each other. "You think the Hawkesbury Monster is real? Let's go find out!"

"Yeah! We'll take my boat! Let's show everyone it's just a load of rubbish," Sam declared, emboldened by bravado and youthful recklessness.

"No! You guys have to listen!" Toby pleaded, desperation rising in his voice. "I saw it! Grandpa and I nearly died! You can't go out there!"

But his friends just laughed. "What's the worst that could happen? Come on, Toby! Don't be a wuss!"

Defeated, Toby watched as they gathered their gear and set off into the night. Fear gnawed at his gut, but he felt powerless to stop them.

That night, as the stars shone brightly above, the boat glided silently across the water. Toby, unable to shake his anxiety, paced back and forth by the riverbank, glancing toward the dark water. Hours passed, and the only sounds were the chirps of crickets and the gentle lapping of waves.

Then came a distant splash, followed by an ominous silence.

"Toby!" A voice called out from the darkness, and he recognized it as Sam's. "Toby, come here! You have to see this!"

Panic surged through him. "No! Get out of the water!" he shouted, but his voice echoed into the void. He watched in horror as shadows danced on the surface, the moonlight glinting off something massive beneath the waves.

"Toby!" Ben's voice rang out, filled with panic. "Help us!"

His heart raced as he sprinted toward the river's edge. "Get back to the boat!" he screamed, desperation clawing at his throat.

But the water churned violently, and then, just as quickly, everything went still. The darkness swallowed their cries, leaving only an eerie calm in its wake.

Toby stood frozen, terror coursing through him. He rushed back to the town, bursting into the pub. "They're gone! Sam and Ben are gone!" he cried, breathless and wide-eyed.

"What do you mean gone?" Jack asked, standing up, concern etched on his face.

"They went out to find the monster! They're not coming back!" Toby's voice cracked with fear.

The room fell silent, the laughter replaced by the gravity of his words. Jack's expression turned serious as he gripped Toby's shoulders. "We have to get the boat and search for them. Now!"

They gathered a few townsfolk, and as they pushed off into the dark waters, a sense of dread enveloped them. The night felt different, heavier, as if the river itself was holding its breath.

"Toby, stay close," Jack instructed, scanning the surface for any sign of movement.

The boat glided silently, but the only sounds were the rippling waters and the muffled cries of night birds. Hours passed with no sign of Sam or Ben.

Just as they were about to turn back, a low growl echoed beneath them, sending chills down Toby's spine. The water erupted again, and there it was—the Hawkesbury Monster, its massive form surfacing in the moonlight.

"No!" Jack yelled, steering the boat away, but it was too late. The creature lunged toward them, and the last thing Toby saw was the glowing eyes before darkness engulfed him.

Days later, the townsfolk searched for Sam and Ben, but they never returned. Whispers filled the air, a blend of fear and disbelief. The old tales had resurfaced, and the story of the Hawkesbury Monster grew with each retelling. As for Toby and Jack, they were forever changed, their warnings lost in the currents of disbelief. The river flowed on, a treacherous beauty hiding secrets within its depths, where the shadows danced and the monster waited for its next curious victims, ever hungry for the thrill of the chase.

3
THE WITCH OF WATTLE CREEK

The sun was just peeking over the horizon as the bus rumbled down the road, packed with excited kids from Oakridge School. Laughter and chatter filled the air, a mix of eager anticipation and nervous energy as they headed to their three-night camp at Wattle Creek.

"Oi, did you hear about the witch that haunts Wattle Creek?" Emily piped up, her curly hair bouncing with every bump in the road.

"Witch? What witch?" Liam, a tall boy with a cheeky grin, leaned closer, intrigued. "You reckon she really eats kids?"

"Of course! Everyone knows that old tale!" Emily insisted, her eyes sparkling with mischief. "They say she lives out in the bush, waiting for kids who wander too far. If you stray off the path, she'll grab ya and never let go!"

"You can't honestly believe that stuff." Jake said, rolling his eyes.

"Oh yeah?" Emily shot back, her voice dropping to a dramatic whisper. "Last year, some kids went missing after wandering off. They say the witch got 'em!"

"Seriously?!" Tom interjected, his eyes wide. "What if she really is out there?"

"Come off it! We're just going camping," Jake scoffed, trying to brush off the tension in the air. "I'm not scared!"

"Yeah, let's go find this witch!" Liam said, his bravado shining through. "What's the worst that could happen?"

"Alright, you lot. How about we meet up after lights out?" Emily suggested, her heart racing at the thought of an adventure.

The group of six—Liam, Jake, Sarah, Emily, Tom, and Mia—nodded in agreement, excitement bubbling as they pulled into the campgrounds. As they unloaded their gear, the sun dipped lower in the sky, casting long shadows across the camp.

Once settled into their cabins, the group gathered around a campfire, roasting marshmallows and sharing stories. But the tale of the witch loomed large over their excitement. Emily, relishing the eerie atmosphere, leaned in closer.

"Alright, everyone," she said, her voice dropping to a conspiratorial whisper. "Legend has it that the witch's cottage is hidden deep in the bush, past the creek. She's got a cauldron and everything!"

"Creepy," Mia whispered, glancing around as if expecting to see the witch appear at any moment. "Do you really think she'll come after us?"

"Not if we stick together," Tom reassured her, though his own voice wavered slightly.

As the sun set, the group's chatter grew quieter, replaced by the sounds of the forest awakening around them. Emily could feel the thrill of adventure coursing through her veins. "We should definitely go find the cottage tonight," she said, eyes sparkling with mischief.

"Yeah, let's do it!" Sarah agreed, her excitement bubbling over. "I'll bring the torch!"

With flashlights in hand, they tiptoed out of their cabins, hearts pounding with a mix of fear and exhilaration. The path into the bush was shadowy, the trees looming overhead like ancient giants.

"Keep it down, will ya?" Mia whispered, glancing nervously over her shoulder. "What if she hears us?"

"Don't be a wuss, Mia!" Jake teased, but there was an edge of anxiety in his tone. "Let's just have a look!"

The group ventured deeper into the bush, the sound of crickets chirping filling the air, but an eerie stillness settled around them. They were far from the camp now, the familiar sounds fading behind them.

"Do you reckon we'll actually find anything?" Tom asked, looking around with growing apprehension.

"Only if you stop chatting!" Emily urged, her voice barely concealing her excitement. "The legend says her cottage is somewhere this way!"

They trudged on, and soon a faint glow flickered in the distance. "What's that?" Sarah whispered, squinting into the darkness.

"Let's check it out," Liam said, stepping forward with determination.

As they approached, they discovered a small, crooked cottage nestled among the trees, its windows dimly lit with a flickering light. Vines crawled up the sides of the building, and an odd, sweet yet musty smell hung in the air.

"This must be it!" Emily gasped, her heart racing. "The witch's cottage!"

"Looks more like a dump," Jake said, trying to sound brave but failing to hide his nerves. "Are you guys sure about this?"

"Too late now!" Liam said, his voice filled with exhilaration. "Let's take a peek."

The group huddled at the door, which creaked open with a soft push. Inside, the walls were lined with odd trinkets—dried herbs hung from the ceiling, and strange bottles filled with colourful liquids cluttered the shelves.

"Creepy," Mia whispered, her eyes darting around the room.

"Oi! Check this out!" Tom exclaimed, pointing to a bubbling cauldron in the corner. "It's like something out of a horror movie!"

"Don't touch anything!" Emily warned, but her voice was drowned out by the excited chatter of the others.

Just then, the door swung shut behind them with a loud bang, making them all jump. "What was that?" Sarah yelped, her flashlight flickering.

"Guys, we should get out of here," Mia said, her voice trembling. "This place gives me the creeps."

"Relax! It's just an old shack," Jake scoffed, though his bravado was fading. "Let's have a look around first."

As they explored, the air grew colder, and an unsettling feeling settled over them. They noticed strange markings etched into the floor, and the atmosphere thickened with an eerie tension.

"Maybe we should—" Emily started, but her words were cut off by a raspy voice from the shadows.

"Who dares enter my home?"

The group froze, hearts racing. An old woman with wild hair and a crooked smile emerged from the darkness, her eyes gleaming with mischief.

"Welcome, welcome! I've been waiting for you!" she cackled, her voice echoing around them.

"Run!" Liam shouted, and they bolted for the door, scrambling past the startled witch. The door creaked open, and they burst into the cool night air, not stopping until they reached their camp.

Breathless and terrified, they collapsed by the fire pit. "Did you see her?" Tom gasped, wide-eyed. "That was definitely a witch!"

"Yeah, I reckon we just stirred up something we shouldn't have," Emily replied, shivering.

"We've gotta tell the teachers," Sarah said, looking around nervously. "What if she follows us?"

They quickly made their way back to their cabins, each kid trying to shake off the fear. Morning came, and the sun rose high, but a sense of dread lingered in the air.

At breakfast, the teachers called the roll. "Liam? Jake? Sarah? Emily? Tom? Mia?" Mrs. Harris checked her clipboard, her brow furrowing. "Wait, where's Mia? And Sarah? And... Jake?"

The kids exchanged worried glances, the events of the night flooding back. "They went out last night! They're missing!" Emily cried, panic rising.

"Missing?" Mrs. Harris repeated, her voice tightening. "We need to search the grounds. Everyone stay here!"

The teachers organised a search party, combing through the bush surrounding the camp. "They couldn't have gone far," Mr. Smith said, though his voice lacked conviction.

Hours passed, and dread settled in like a thick fog. Despite their efforts, there was no sign of Mia, Sarah, or Jake. The sun began to set, casting an orange glow over the treetops, and a chill crept into the air.

"We need to call the police," Mrs. Harris said, her voice shaking. "This isn't good."

As night fell, the school camp was enveloped in darkness, the once cheerful atmosphere replaced by an unsettling silence. The police arrived and organised a larger search party, their flashlights slicing through the inky blackness of the bush.

"Maybe they just got lost," one officer suggested, but doubt lingered in his eyes.

"We can't rule out anything," the lead officer replied grimly. "Let's keep searching."

Hours turned into a restless night, but there was still no sign of the missing kids. The campfire flickered and dimmed, and the woods seemed to close in around them. The legend of the witch hung heavy in the air, and the sounds of the forest felt more menacing than before.

In the distance, a low, haunting cackle echoed, sending shivers down everyone's spines.

"Did you hear that?" one of the officers whispered, his face paling.

"Yeah... it sounded like..." Mrs. Harris trailed off, unable to finish her sentence.

The forest was alive with the noise of unseen creatures, and the witch's legend had transformed from a mere story into a chilling reality. As the search continued, it became clear: the bush was concealing more than just the missing kids. The witch was real, and the darkness of Wattle Creek held onto its secrets tightly. As the night deepened, the fire sputtered and dimmed, and the woods seemed to close in around the camp. The stories that once felt like harmless fun now echoed with a chilling truth—some legends were born from fear, and others were simply waiting to be told.

4

THE HAUNTING OF MANLY STATION

It was a warm October evening when the Donaldson family arrived at the Manly Quarantine Station. The sun was setting behind the waves, casting long shadows that danced ominously on the ground. Nine-year-old Amy clutched her flashlight, eyes sparkling with excitement, while her older brother, Sam, tried to hide his nerves behind a brave facade.

"C'mon, Dad! This is gonna be epic!" Amy exclaimed, her voice echoing slightly in the twilight.

"Epic? More like a waste of time," their dad, Rob, replied, crossing his arms. "Ghosts aren't real, kids. Just stories to scare you silly."

Mum, Sarah, rolled her eyes. "You said you'd give it a go, Rob. Just keep an open mind. For the kids' sake."

"Yeah, Dad! You might even see a ghost!" Sam added, trying to sound enthusiastic while secretly wishing he'd stayed home.

As they joined the small group gathered outside the old quarantine station, a chill swept through the air, making Amy shiver. The tour guide, a tall man with a tattered coat and a wide-brimmed hat, began speaking in a low, eerie tone.

"Welcome to Manly Quarantine Station, a place filled with stories of the past, where the spirits of those who never left may still roam. Keep your eyes peeled, and your wits about you."

Rob scoffed under his breath. "Right, as if!"

"Shh! Listen," Amy hissed, nudging her dad. "What if we see something?"

The guide led them through the dimly lit pathways, the air thick with the scent of salt and decay. Shadows flickered in the corners of their vision, and every now and then, a soft moan seemed to echo from the old buildings.

"Did you hear that?" Sam whispered, glancing nervously at Amy.

"Yeah, sounds like a ghost!" Amy replied, giggling nervously.

"More likely the wind," Rob muttered, but his voice lacked conviction.

As they entered one of the main buildings, the guide told them about the tragic history of the quarantine station, where ill-fated passengers had been kept isolated during disease outbreaks.

"A few of them died here," the guide explained, his voice dropping to a whisper. "And many say their spirits still linger, waiting for someone to tell their stories."

Rob rolled his eyes again, but the rest of the family was captivated. They walked through dark hallways, the wooden floors creaking beneath their feet. Suddenly, Amy felt a cold breeze brush against her cheek, making her shiver.

"Did you feel that?" she gasped.

"Stop it, Amy!" Rob said, trying to sound tough. "It's just a draft."

But as they moved deeper into the station, the atmosphere changed. The air grew colder, and an unsettling feeling settled over them. They entered a large room filled with old medical equipment and dusty furniture.

"Now, this is creepy," Sam admitted, glancing around. "Maybe Dad's right about ghosts."

Just then, the lights flickered, casting eerie shadows that danced on the walls. Amy's heart raced, and she clutched Sam's arm. "What's happening?"

The guide smiled mysteriously. "Sometimes the spirits like to make their presence known. They're curious about you."

"Yeah, right," Rob scoffed, but there was a slight tremor in his voice now.

"Come on, Dad! Just chill!" Amy urged. "Let's see what happens."

As they continued the tour, they entered a narrow corridor lined with old photographs of patients. The guide pointed out a particular picture. "This is Mary, a young girl who passed away here. People say she's often seen wandering these halls, looking for her family."

Just then, a cold gust of wind rushed through the corridor, extinguishing their flashlights momentarily. Panic surged as the darkness enveloped them.

"Everyone stay calm!" the guide shouted, his voice steady. "Just wait for the lights to come back on."

As the lights flickered back to life, Amy noticed that Rob was missing. "Dad? Where are you?" she called, her voice echoing in the sudden stillness.

"He must have gone to the bathroom or something," Sam said, but his tone betrayed his uncertainty.

"Yeah, but he would've told us!" Amy insisted, glancing down the dark corridor. "Let's find him."

"Let's just stick with the group," Sam replied, but Amy had already started walking back.

As they retraced their steps, a heavy silence fell over the station. The guide had moved on with the group, and Amy felt a gnawing sense of dread in her stomach.

"Dad!" she called again, louder this time. "Where are you?"

They reached the main hall, but there was no sign of Rob. "This isn't funny!" Amy shouted, panic creeping into her voice.

"Maybe he went outside," Sam suggested, but he didn't sound convinced.

Just then, a soft whisper floated through the air, sending chills down their spines. "Help me... find me..."

"Did you hear that?" Amy asked, her voice trembling.

"Yeah, but it's probably just the wind," Sam replied, though he looked frightened.

"Let's check outside," Amy insisted, tugging on Sam's sleeve. They stepped out into the open air, the cool breeze wrapping around them like a ghostly embrace.

"Dad!" they shouted together, but the only response was the distant crashing of waves.

Suddenly, a figure appeared at the edge of the trees, half-hidden in the shadows. It looked like Rob, but something was off. He stood still, staring blankly into the darkness.

"Dad?" Sam called hesitantly. "What are you doing?"

But Rob didn't respond. Instead, he slowly raised a hand, pointing into the trees.

"Dad!" Amy screamed, her heart pounding. "Come back!"

As they rushed toward him, the figure turned and melted into the shadows, disappearing before their eyes. The kids skidded to a halt, panic surging through them.

"Where did he go?" Sam asked, his voice trembling.

"I don't know!" Amy cried, her eyes wide with fear. "We have to find him!"

They darted back into the station, calling for their dad, but every room was empty, echoing their voices back at them. The eerie feeling settled heavier in the air, and shadows seemed to close in around them.

"Maybe we should go back to the group," Sam suggested, glancing nervously at the dark corners of the building.

"Yeah, but what if Dad's in trouble?" Amy insisted, fighting back tears. "We can't just leave him!"

Just then, they heard a soft sobbing sound coming from the medical room. "Is that... Dad?" Sam whispered, his heart racing.

They moved cautiously toward the sound. As they entered, the room was empty except for the dust and shadows. The sobbing stopped abruptly, replaced by the chilling whisper again, "Help me... find me..."

"Where are you?" Amy cried out, desperation in her voice.

Suddenly, the lights flickered again, and in that brief moment of darkness, they saw a shadow dart past them. When the lights came back on, Rob was still nowhere to be found.

"Let's get out of here!" Sam shouted, his voice rising in panic.

They rushed outside, their breath visible in the cold night air. As they reached the open space, Amy turned back toward the station, feeling a pull to go inside once more. "We can't leave him!"

Just then, the wind howled, and an icy mist enveloped the area. Amy and Sam stood frozen, watching as the mist swirled and began to form shapes—figures of lost souls emerging from the shadows.

"Help us..." they whispered in unison, their voices haunting.

"Run!" Sam yelled, grabbing Amy's hand as they sprinted away from the station, the sobbing echoing in their ears.

As they reached the beach, they turned to look back one last time. The quarantine station stood dark and foreboding, the mist swirling ominously around it.

"Dad!" Amy screamed, but the only response was the crashing waves and the wind.

In the days that followed, the Donaldson family searched tirelessly for Rob, but he was never found. The ghost tour had ended with a grim reality—he had vanished without a trace, leaving Amy and Sam to grapple with a haunting truth.

"Do you think... do you think he's a ghost now?" Amy whispered one night, her voice trembling.

Sam nodded slowly, tears in his eyes. "Maybe he's still looking for us, like the others..."

And as they sat in the dark, the whispers of the quarantine station echoed in their minds, a chilling reminder that some spirits never find their way home.

5

THE TROLL UNDER RICHMOND BRIDGE

On Halloween night, under a sliver of a moon, three friends crept out of their houses in the quiet town of Richmond, Tasmania. The air was cool and crisp, and the trees whispered secrets as they walked. Josh, Mia, and Ben had heard the stories about the old Richmond Bridge—the one that stood stoic and crumbling, rumoured to be haunted by a ghostly figure who roamed the night.

"Oi, what if the stories are true?" Mia whispered, her eyes wide with excitement and fear.

"Don't be a sook," Ben scoffed, rolling his eyes. "It's just a load of rubbish. Ghosts ain't real."

Josh chuckled, adjusting his backpack. "What if we find something even better? Like a troll or something?"

"A troll?" Mia raised an eyebrow, smirking. "Like a big, ugly one? C'mon, mate, that's just a fairytale."

"Yeah, but imagine if it's real," Josh said, grinning. "We could be legends!"

The trio made their way down to the bridge, the old stones looming ahead like the fangs of a giant. The bridge was built in 1823 and was said to be one of the oldest in Australia, but tonight, it looked more like a scene from a horror film.

"Let's get a move on, yeah?" Ben urged, nervously glancing around. "I reckon we should stick together. This place gives me the creeps."

Mia nodded, her heart racing. "Right, so what's the plan?"

"We check it out, have a laugh, then head home," Josh declared, stepping forward. "No backing out now!"

As they approached the bridge, the wind howled, and shadows danced in the flickering light of their torches. They could hear the gentle trickle of the river beneath them, but it did little to ease the tension.

"Anyone else feeling a bit dodgy?" Ben asked, his voice trembling slightly.

"Stop being such a wuss," Mia shot back. "You wanted to come, remember?"

"Yeah, but I didn't think it'd be this scary!" he replied, glancing over his shoulder.

"Alright, let's just cross the bridge," Josh said, trying to sound brave. "Then we'll have a squiz under it."

They stepped onto the bridge, the stones cold beneath their feet. As they walked, the creaking of the old structure echoed in the still night. Suddenly, Mia halted, shining her torch into the dark.

"Did you hear that?" she whispered.

"Hear what?" Ben asked, squinting into the shadows.

"It sounded like... growling," Mia said, her voice shaky.

"Growling? You've been reading too many scary stories!" Josh laughed nervously, though he too felt a chill run down his spine.

As they reached the middle of the bridge, they paused to peer over the edge. The water flowed swiftly below, but what caught their attention was a dark shape lurking beneath the bridge.

"Oi, look!" Josh exclaimed, pointing. "Is that... something moving?"

The three of them leaned closer, and as the beam of their torches illuminated the darkness, they saw a hulking figure. It was enormous, covered in matted green fur, with eyes that glowed like two fiery coals.

"That's not a ghost!" Mia shrieked. "That's a troll!"

"A troll? You're joking!" Ben's voice was high-pitched with fear.

"Let's get outta here!" he yelled, but it was too late. The troll let out a low growl and rose to its full height, towering over them.

"Who dares disturb my peace?" the troll bellowed, its voice rumbling like thunder.

The three friends stood frozen, their hearts pounding in their chests.

"Um, we... we were just exploring!" Josh stammered, trying to sound brave. "We didn't mean any harm!"

The troll stepped closer, revealing its grotesque face, with jagged teeth and a long, crooked nose. "Exploring, eh? You kids are trespassing on my turf! Do you have any idea what I do to trespassers?"

Mia stepped forward, her fear slowly melting into defiance. "What are you gonna do? Eat us for dinner?"

The troll snorted, a mix of laughter and disgust. "I'm not some silly monster from a bedtime story! I'm a guardian of this bridge. People come to me for help, not for a midnight scare."

"Help? You?" Ben echoed, still trembling. "What kind of help do you give?"

"Ah, so you're curious!" the troll grinned, revealing more of its sharp teeth. "I help those who've lost their way or need guidance. But you lot? You've come here with no respect. So what do you want?"

Josh, feeling a surge of courage, stepped up. "We wanted to see if the stories about ghosts were true."

The troll's eyes narrowed. "Ghosts? They're a myth! I'm the real deal, and if you've come for stories, I've got plenty to tell."

Mia exchanged glances with Ben and Josh, her curiosity piqued. "Alright, then. Tell us your best story."

The troll scratched its chin, considering them. "Very well. But first, you must promise to respect the bridge and its history."

"We promise," Josh said quickly.

"Alright," the troll began, its voice now softer. "Long ago, before this bridge was built, a great flood swept through the valley. Many people lost their homes. I saved a little girl who was lost, bringing her to safety under this very bridge. She told the townsfolk of my kindness, and they built the bridge in my honour."

"Wow," Mia said, eyes wide. "I never knew that!"

"But that's not all," the troll continued, his tone shifting to something more serious. "The spirits of those who perished in the flood still roam the area, and sometimes they ask for help too. That's why I keep watch—because not everyone is as brave as you three."

Ben looked at his friends, awe replacing his fear. "So you're not a monster at all!"

The troll chuckled, a deep rumble that echoed off the stones. "No, but people fear what they don't understand. You'd be surprised how many come here for help, even if they're too scared to admit it."

Josh, now feeling a bond forming, said, "We're sorry for trespassing. We didn't know you were guarding the place."

"Apology accepted," the troll grinned. "But remember, next time you come to the bridge, come as friends—not intruders."

"Deal," Mia said, smiling. "Can we tell our friends about you?"

"Only if you make sure they respect the bridge as you have," the troll replied, a twinkle in its eyes. "Now, go home before the spirits come out to play!"

With a new understanding of their unlikely friend, the three friends scampered off the bridge, their hearts lighter and laughter bubbling up as they shared their adventure.

"Next Halloween, we'll come back," Josh said, looking back at the bridge, now a beacon of mystery and friend-ship.

"Yeah," Ben added, still buzzing from the thrill. "But let's bring snacks this time!"

"Good idea!" Mia said, her excitement rekindled. "And maybe a story to share!"

As they walked away, the troll watched them, a knowing smile on its face, keeping the bridge safe for generations to come.

6

THE LEGEND OF THE BUSH WITCH

It was a clear night in the Australian bush, and five friends had gathered for a weekend of camping beneath the stars. The flickering bonfire cast shadows on their faces as they roasted marshmallows and shared stories, laughter mingling with the crackling of the fire.

"Alright, who's up for a spooky story?" Jake challenged, his eyes glinting with mischief.

"Not this again!" Sarah groaned, rolling her eyes. "Last time you told a ghost story, I couldn't sleep!"

"Come on, it's Halloween weekend! You can't just sit here and tell fairy tales," Jake teased. "I'll start. Have you guys heard about the Bush Witch?"

"Oh great, here we go," said Liam, leaning back against a log.

"Shush! This is a classic," Jake insisted, his voice dropping to a whisper. "They say she lives deep in the bush, and if you wander too far, she'll find you. She's got long black hair that drags on the ground, and she's ancient and twisted. But the worst part? She eats children to stay young forever!"

"Shut up, mate! You're just trying to scare us," Sarah said, half-laughing but glancing nervously at the dark trees surrounding them.

"No, really! People say she lures kids away with her sweet singing. If you hear her voice, it's already too late. She's got a cabin hidden away where she does... stuff," Jake said, wiggling his fingers for effect.

"'Stuff'? What stuff?" Emma asked, leaning in closer.

"Witchy stuff! Potions and spells. They say if she catches you, you'll never come back," Jake said, his voice low and eerie. "You'll end up just another lost soul in the bush."

"Sounds like a load of rubbish," Liam muttered, trying to sound brave.

But as the fire crackled and the shadows danced, a chill crept through the air. The friends exchanged nervous glances, the legend of the Bush Witch lingering heavily in the atmosphere.

"Let's find her," Sarah blurted out, surprising everyone. "What if we can actually find her cabin?"

"Seriously? You want to go looking for a witch?" Jake laughed, though a hint of fear flickered in his eyes.

"Why not? We've got flashlights, and it'll be fun!" Sarah insisted, her excitement bubbling over. "Just think of the adventure!"

"I'm in," said Emma, eyes sparkling with thrill. "What do we have to lose?"

Liam sighed. "Alright, but if we get eaten by a witch, I'm blaming you, Sarah."

With their minds made up, the group finished their marshmallows and prepared for an adventure. As they made their way into the bush, the trees loomed taller, their branches swaying like skeletal fingers in the breeze. The sounds of the night grew louder—the rustling leaves, distant animal calls, and the ever-present hum of the bush.

"Keep your eyes peeled for anything weird," Jake said, trying to sound brave but failing to hide his nervousness.

After walking for what felt like an eternity, they stumbled upon a small, dilapidated cabin hidden among the trees. It was dark and weathered, vines creeping up the walls as if trying to reclaim it.

"This must be it!" Sarah exclaimed, her voice echoing in the stillness.

"Or it's a haunted shack where we'll all get stuck forever," Liam said, rolling his eyes but stepping closer.
"Let's check it out," Emma said, her curiosity piqued.
"We're already here."
As they approached, the door creaked open slightly, as
if inviting them inside. Jake took a deep breath and
nudged it further open. "After you, brave souls!"
Inside, the air was thick with dust and the scent of decay. The cabin was cluttered with odd trinkets and herbs
hanging from the ceiling, their dried forms swaying gently
in the breeze.
"Yuck! What's that smell?" Liam wrinkled his nose.
"Probably the witch's cooking," Sarah joked, but her
voice wavered.
"Let's not hang around too long," Jake suggested. "We
don't want to annoy the Bush Witch."
As they explored the cabin, they found old books filled
with strange symbols and handwritten notes. Emma
picked one up, flipping through the pages. "Look at this! It
talks about potions and—"
"—and curses," Liam interrupted, pointing at a drawing
of a woman with long black hair. "That's her!"
"Maybe we should get out of here," Sarah said, feeling
uneasy.
But before they could leave, a soft humming filled the
air, a haunting melody that sent shivers down their
spines. The sound seemed to come from behind a closed
door at the back of the cabin.
"Do you hear that?" Emma asked, her eyes wide.
"Yeah, and it's creeping me out," Jake replied, backing
away slowly.

"Let's see what it is," Sarah urged, her curiosity getting the better of her. She walked toward the door, her hand trembling as she reached for the knob.

"Are you mental? We shouldn't go in there!" Liam protested, grabbing her arm.

But Sarah twisted the knob and pushed the door open. Inside was a dark room filled with jars—each one filled with something unidentifiable. The humming grew louder, filling the room with a chilling energy.

Suddenly, the door slammed shut behind them, and they spun around in panic. The air turned cold, and shadows began to swirl in the corners of the room.

"Let us out!" Jake shouted, banging on the door, but it wouldn't budge.

The humming morphed into a chilling laugh, echoing around them. "You're just in time for dinner!" a voice called out, raspy and old.

"What do you want with us?" Emma cried, backing away as the shadows seemed to stretch and twist.

"Why, to join my collection, of course," the voice hissed. "You're just the right age. So full of life!"

"No way! We're not going to be your next meal!" Liam shouted, panic rising.

"Then you should have stayed away from my home!" The shadows coiled closer, and a figure emerged, long black hair trailing like tendrils behind her.

"It's the Bush Witch!" Sarah screamed, terror gripping her heart.

With a surge of adrenaline, Jake charged at the door, but it wouldn't budge. "We have to find a way out!" he yelled.

The witch cackled, her eyes glowing with a sinister light. "You think you can escape? You're in my domain now!"

The friends huddled together, hearts racing as they searched for a way out. "We can't just stand here!" Emma shouted. "We have to do something!"

Liam spotted a window, partially open, and pointed. "There! We can climb out!"

"Quick!" Sarah urged, and they scrambled toward the window, pushing each other through in a frenzy. Just as they climbed out, the witch let out an ear-piercing scream, shaking the walls of the cabin.

"Come back!" she shrieked, but they didn't look back. They ran through the bush, hearts pounding, branches clawing at them like the witch's fingers. They sprinted until they reached the clearing where their campfire still flickered in the distance.

"Go, go, go!" Jake yelled, urging the others forward. Once they reached the safety of their camp, they collapsed onto the ground, panting and shaking. The fire felt warm and inviting, a stark contrast to the horrors they had just escaped.

"What was that?" Emma gasped, glancing back at the dark woods.

"The Bush Witch," Liam breathed, still wide-eyed. "She's real! We were almost..."

"No! We're not going to think about that," Jake said firmly. "We made it out. That's what matters."

As they sat huddled around the fire, they couldn't shake the feeling that they were being watched. The night seemed to grow darker, and the wind whispered through the trees, carrying the faintest echo of the witch's haunting laughter.

"Maybe we should just pack up and go home," Sarah suggested, looking nervously into the shadows.

But just as they began to gather their things, a chill swept through the camp. A shadow flickered at the edge of the firelight, and they heard the soft, eerie hum once more.

"Help me... find me..." the voice drifted through the air, sending a fresh wave of terror coursing through them.

As they turned to face the darkness, the bush whispered their secrets, and the legend of the Bush Witch lived on—waiting for the next unsuspecting campers to wander too close to her cabin in the woods.

7

THE LAST BLACK JADE

In the opulent suburb of Toorak, where grand mansions loomed like ancient sentinels and manicured gardens flourished under the Australian sun, there existed a hidden treasure that few knew about: the last black jade, said to hold immense power and an ancient curse.

Among the residents was a young art historian named Clara, who had recently returned from studying abroad. Her curiosity about the mysterious legends of Toorak led her to uncover tales of the black jade—a stone once owned by a wealthy family that mysteriously vanished from the area decades ago. Whispers spoke of its beauty and the tragedy that followed its last known possession.

One chilly evening, drawn by an insatiable curiosity, Clara found herself wandering through the dimly lit streets. The moon hung low, casting an eerie glow on the opulent facades. As she passed the old manor known as the Murchison House, she felt an inexplicable pull towards it. The house was a local legend, rumoured to be haunted by the spirits of the family who had owned the black jade.

"Hey, Clara!" called out her friend Liam, catching up to her. "What are you doing out here?"

"I'm just exploring," she replied, glancing back at the imposing structure. "Have you ever heard about the black jade?"

Liam shivered, pulling his jacket tighter around himself. "Yeah, they say it brings misfortune. You shouldn't mess with that stuff. The Murchison family went missing after they found it."

"I need to know more," Clara insisted. "I think there might be a connection to an old painting I've been studying."

With a reluctant nod, Liam agreed to accompany her, albeit hesitantly. As they approached the house, a sudden gust of wind rattled the trees, and Clara felt a chill crawl up her spine.

"Are you sure about this?" Liam asked, glancing around nervously.

"Just a quick look," Clara replied, her heart racing with excitement and fear.

The front door creaked open with an ominous groan as they pushed it ajar. The interior was shrouded in dust and cobwebs, but remnants of luxury remained: ornate chandeliers hung from the ceiling, and faded portraits of the Murchison family lined the walls. Clara's eyes fell on a particularly striking portrait of a woman adorned in jewels, her gaze hauntingly intense.

"Look at this," Clara said, stepping closer. "She looks just like the descriptions of the last owner. I think her name was Evelyn."

Liam peered over Clara's shoulder, and a cold breeze swept through the room, causing him to shudder. "Let's find that jade and get out of here."

They wandered through the house, the floorboards creaking beneath their feet. As they made their way to the library, Clara spotted a glimmering object half-buried under a pile of old books.

"Is that it?" she gasped, reaching down. She unearthed a small box, intricately carved, and covered in dust. With trembling hands, she opened it, revealing a piece of black jade, polished to a glossy finish. It seemed to pulse with an energy that was both alluring and terrifying.

"Clara, put it down!" Liam warned, his voice a mix of fear and urgency.

But she was entranced. "It's beautiful. I need to take it with me."

As she held the jade, the air around them grew thick, and the temperature plummeted. Shadows flickered in the corners of the room, and a low whisper echoed through the halls. "Leave... now..."

"What was that?" Liam shouted, backing away.

Clara dropped the jade back into the box, her heart racing. "We need to go. Now."

They fled the library, but the house seemed to shift around them. The hallways elongated, the portraits on the walls appearing to watch them with accusatory eyes. As they turned a corner, Clara felt an icy hand grip her wrist.

"Clara!" Liam screamed, pulling her away from the unseen force.

The whispers intensified, drowning out their panic. "You've awakened us... you must pay the price..."

With desperation, they rushed towards the front door, but it slammed shut before they could reach it. The atmosphere thickened, the shadows deepening into a darkness that seemed alive.

"Let us out!" Clara cried, banging on the door, but it wouldn't budge.

In that moment of sheer terror, the whispers transformed into anguished wails, echoing around them. The very walls seemed to vibrate with pain and sorrow. "The jade is ours! You cannot leave!"

Liam turned to Clara, his eyes wide with panic. "What do we do?"

Clara remembered the painting—the woman's intense gaze held a sorrowful depth. "We need to return it!" she shouted, grabbing the box. "It's the only way!"

With determination, they sprinted back to the library, the oppressive darkness chasing them. As they reached the room, Clara hurled the box containing the jade onto the dusty table.

"Please!" she shouted. "We're sorry! We didn't mean to disturb you!"

The air crackled with energy, and the shadows swirled around them, coalescing into the figure of Evelyn Murchison, her face twisted in anguish. "You have taken what is mine!"

"No!" Clara cried, backing away. "We're returning it! Please, let us go!"

Evelyn's eyes softened for a moment, glistening with tears. "The jade binds us to this world. Its power has trapped our souls. Only by returning it can we find peace."

Liam stepped forward, trembling. "We'll help you. Just let us leave."

With a flick of her hand, the shadows receded slightly. "Place the jade upon my portrait. Only then will we be free."

Clara nodded, her heart racing. They hurried back to the portrait, the box clutched tightly in Clara's hands. As they approached, the whispers grew louder, the air vibrating with urgency.

"Quick!" Liam urged.

With trembling fingers, Clara opened the box and lifted the jade, feeling its weight—both physical and metaphysical—as she set it against the frame of the painting. The moment it touched the surface, a blinding light erupted, and the room shook violently.

Evelyn's spirit appeared before them, her expression a mixture of relief and sorrow. "Thank you," she whispered, her voice fading. "You have freed us."

As the light consumed them, Clara and Liam felt an overwhelming sense of calm wash over them. The wails faded, replaced by a gentle breeze that lifted the darkness from the house.

When the light subsided, they found themselves outside the mansion, the moon now shining brightly above. The air felt fresh, and the oppressive weight had lifted.

"What just happened?" Liam breathed, his heart still racing.

"I think... I think we freed them," Clara replied, still in shock. "The jade was the source of their suffering."

As they turned to look at the mansion, it appeared ordinary, the shadows retreating into the night. But Clara knew the truth—the last black jade had held a power far beyond what she had ever imagined.

From that night on, the stories of the Murchison family faded, becoming just another legend of Toorak. But Clara and Liam would never forget the darkness they had faced, nor the sacrifice they had made to bring light back to the shadows.

8
BIG GARRY

Based on actual events

It was a warm summer night in 1975, and the air was thick with mischief as a group of teenage boys wandered the streets of Newtown, Sydney. The school holidays had just begun, and the gang was looking for trouble.

"Oi, let's check out the cemetery!" John shouted, his eyes gleaming with excitement. The others, Sam, Dave, and Tom, exchanged glances, unsure.

"Are you serious?" Sam said, his voice wavering. "You know what they say about that place—ghosts and all that."

"Come on! It'll be a laugh!" John insisted, egging them on. "And we can mess with Big Garry! He's just an old bloke with an axe."

"Yeah, but he's creepy," Dave replied, shivering despite the heat.

"Don't be a sook!" John shot back. "What's he gonna do? He's just a grumpy grave digger."

Reluctantly, the boys followed John down the dimly lit streets towards Newtown Cemetery, one of the oldest in Australia. The moon hung high, casting eerie shadows among the old gravestones as they pushed through the wrought-iron gates.

"Look at this place!" Tom whispered, his voice filled with awe and dread. The cemetery was overgrown, with weeds creeping up the sides of weathered tombstones. The atmosphere felt thick, almost alive.

"Let's find Big Garry!" John said, a mischievous grin plastered across his face. "I bet he's lurking around here somewhere."

As they ventured deeper into the cemetery, the boys began to hear the sounds of rustling leaves and distant hoots of owls. John, full of bravado, shouted, "Hey, Garry! We know you're out here! Come on, show yourself!"

"Shhh!" Sam hissed. "What if he actually hears you?"

"Relax, it's just an old man," John scoffed, waving his hand dismissively. "Besides, he can't be that scary."

Suddenly, a rustling sound echoed from behind a nearby tombstone. The boys froze, their hearts pounding. Out of the shadows emerged a tall figure, silhouetted against the moonlight, clutching something shiny.

"Who dares disturb my work?" a deep voice growled.

"Big Garry!" Tom exclaimed, his eyes wide with terror. "Run!"

But John, feeling brave, stood his ground. "We're not afraid of you, Garry!" he shouted. "You can't scare us!"

The figure stepped forward, revealing an imposing man with a scraggly beard and wild hair, his eyes glinting like steel. In his hand, he held an old axe, the moonlight glinting ominously off its blade.

"You boys think this is a joke?" Big Garry said, his voice low and gravelly. "This is sacred ground. You need to leave."

"Make us!" John taunted, puffing out his chest. The other boys looked at him in disbelief, their fear palpable.

"John, don't!" Sam pleaded. "Let's just go."

But John wasn't listening. He stepped closer to Big Garry, a grin on his face. "What are you gonna do? Chase us away with your axe?"

Big Garry's expression darkened. "You think I'm playing games?" He swung the axe lightly, the metal slicing through the air. "Leave now, or you'll regret it."

The boys exchanged frightened looks, and for a moment, silence enveloped them. Then, with a sudden burst of adrenaline, John shouted, "You can't scare us! We're not afraid of you!"

Big Garry's eyes narrowed, and with a terrifying roar, he lunged forward. The boys screamed and scattered, running in different directions.

"Stick together!" Dave shouted, but the darkness seemed to swallow their voices. John led the charge, but his bravado quickly turned to panic as he realised he had strayed too far from the group.

"Guys! Where are you?" John yelled, his voice echoing in the stillness. He stumbled over roots and tombstones, fear pounding in his chest. He could hear Big Garry's footsteps behind him, heavy and relentless.

John ducked behind a large gravestone, panting. "What do I do?" he whispered to himself, glancing around. Suddenly, he felt something cold against his neck—a chill that sent shivers down his spine.

"Thought you could run from me?" Big Garry's voice growled, close enough that John could feel his breath. The axe glinted menacingly in the moonlight.

"Please, I didn't mean it!" John begged, realising too late that he had gone too far. "I was just joking!"

Big Garry stepped closer, towering over him. "This is not a joke, boy. You disrespected the dead, and now you must pay the price."

In a flash, John turned to bolt, but he stumbled, falling to the ground. He looked up, his heart racing as he saw Big Garry raise the axe.

"Stop!" cried a voice from the darkness. It was Sam, Tom, and Dave, their faces pale with fear. "Leave him alone, Garry!"

The sight of his friends gave John a surge of hope. "Help!" he shouted, scrambling to his feet.

"Get out of here!" Sam urged, eyes wide. "We didn't mean to disturb you!"

Big Garry paused, his gaze shifting between the boys. "You think I care for your pleas?" He took a step back, then pointed the axe at them. "If you don't leave now, you'll all suffer the same fate!"

"Come on, John! Let's go!" Tom shouted, grabbing John by the arm. The boys didn't wait for another word; they sprinted back through the maze of gravestones, their hearts pounding, the echo of Big Garry's voice trailing behind them.

"Foolish children!" he bellowed. "You'll never escape your fate!"

Bursting through the cemetery gates, the boys didn't stop running until they reached the street, panting and terrified. They turned to look back at the cemetery, now looming dark and silent behind them.

"Did that really just happen?" Sam gasped, trying to catch his breath.

"Yeah, and we were stupid to mess with him," John said, shaking. "I thought he was just some old codger."

"Let's never come back here," Dave said, wide-eyed. "That was too close."

As they walked away, the moonlight cast long shadows behind them, and in the distance, they could have sworn they heard a deep, haunting laugh echoing through the trees. The boys knew they had narrowly escaped a fate worse than they could ever have imagined. The old cemetery held secrets they weren't ready to face—and Big Garry was a guardian of those secrets, waiting for the next group of reckless kids to wander in.

9
THE TALL MAN IN THE TOWER

On a warm summer evening in Windsor, New South Wales, a gentle breeze rustled the leaves of the ancient trees lining the streets. The air was thick with the scent of eucalyptus, and the sky painted shades of pink and orange as Lucy Bennett, a woman in her mid-thirties, took her usual evening stroll with her dog, Arlo. The two of them had walked this same route every evening for the past year, and the quiet, sleepy town of Windsor had become familiar, even comforting.

Lucy lived in a little cottage near the heart of town. Each evening, as the sun dipped behind the hills, she'd leash Arlo and head toward the old cemetery that sat just on the edge of town, where the crumbling stone walls and crooked, weather-worn tombstones told stories of long-forgotten lives.

The cemetery was one of the oldest in Australia, dating back to the early 1800s. It was a place of both reverence and mystery. Many of the graves were overgrown, and some of the stones were so worn by time that they could barely be read. But the most curious thing about the cemetery was the old church that stood at the centre, with its tall, narrow spire that reached for the sky. The church had been abandoned for decades, and no one dared to go inside. There were whispers among the townsfolk that it was haunted by the figure of a tall man, someone no one could identify, who had been seen standing at the top of the tower at night.

Lucy had always felt uneasy as she walked past the cemetery. There was something about it—the way the wind seemed to moan through the trees, the way the shadows seemed to stretch and shift in the fading light—that made her skin crawl. But she'd never thought much of it. After all, she was a practical woman. Ghost stories were just that: stories. Or so she thought.

This particular evening, as Lucy and Arlo reached the cemetery gates, something felt different. It wasn't the usual chill that brushed the back of her neck. It was something more—something she couldn't quite put her finger on.

Arlo, usually so calm and collected, tugged at his leash, growling low in his throat.

"Shh, it's alright, Arlo," Lucy murmured, patting his head. She thought it might be a possum or some other small creature in the bushes, but Arlo's behaviour only grew more anxious. He pulled toward the gates, ears pricked, and tail stiff.

Lucy frowned. She had passed this place a hundred times before, but tonight, something was... off.

As she stood at the edge of the cemetery, her gaze shifted up to the tall church spire. Her heart skipped a beat. The light at the top of the tower was on.

The church had been abandoned for as long as anyone could remember, and yet every night, without fail, the light was there. It had become a strange, eerie fixture in the town, one that no one could explain. The light burned with an unnatural glow, casting long shadows across the cemetery, and yet no one had ever dared to investigate why.

Lucy had heard the stories—the stories of the tall man who haunted the church tower. The stories were always the same: a tall, shadowy figure standing at the top, watching over the town. No one knew who he was or where he came from, but the town's elders warned that he was not to be disturbed.

But tonight, Lucy couldn't shake the feeling that something more was going on. She felt an odd pull, as if the light was calling to her, beckoning her closer.

"Arlo, stay!" she commanded as he pulled at the leash, but Arlo was already off, darting toward the gates. Lucy had no choice but to follow.

As they walked deeper into the cemetery, the wind grew still, the air thick with the scent of damp earth. The old tombstones loomed above them, casting long, jagged shadows across the ground.

Then, it came. A sound, faint at first, but unmistakable... a baby's cry.

Lucy stopped in her tracks, heart racing. Arlo barked in the direction of the sound, his hackles raised. The cry echoed through the graveyard, distant but close, as if it was coming from within the church.

"Where is that coming from?" Lucy whispered, her voice barely audible.

The sound of a baby crying at the old church tower? It made no sense. The church had been abandoned for years.

Arlo continued to bark and tug at the leash, eager to move forward. Lucy hesitated, the hairs on the back of her neck standing on end. But the cry—so heartbreaking and sorrowful—pulled at her.

"Arlo, wait!" she said, but Arlo had already bolted toward the church.

Lucy had no choice but to follow. Her heart thudded in her chest as she moved through the cemetery, passing tombstones that seemed to watch her as she walked. The sound of the baby's cry grew louder with every step, the sorrow in it undeniable. It was as if it was coming from behind the church doors themselves.

When Lucy reached the church, she stopped at the heavy wooden door. It was old, weathered, and locked. But something in her gut told her the door might not stay locked for long.

Suddenly, the cry stopped.

A cold gust of wind swept through the cemetery, carrying with it the faint sound of footsteps. They were slow, deliberate, as if someone—no, something—was walking toward her.

Lucy spun around, her heart in her throat. Out of the corner of her eye, she saw a tall, shadowy figure at the top of the church tower. The tall man.

Her breath caught in her throat as the figure seemed to stare down at her from the tower. His silhouette was indistinct, but his presence was unmistakable. He was watching her, waiting.

Before she could react, a voice, soft and almost apologetic, drifted toward her.

"You shouldn't be here," it said.

Lucy whipped around, but no one was there. Arlo stood at her side, whimpering.

"You shouldn't be here," the voice repeated, a little more forceful this time.

It was then that Lucy understood—the tall man wasn't just a ghost. He was the protector of the cemetery, the guardian of the secrets buried there. And the baby's cry? It wasn't a child. It was a warning—a lure to bring the curious closer, to keep them from trespassing into the church where forbidden things slept.

Lucy took a step back, feeling the pull of the cemetery's dark secrets. But as she turned to leave, the church bell tolled—loud and deep—echoing across the land.

Lucy didn't look back again. With Arlo by her side, she quickly left the cemetery, the wind howling behind her, and the light in the tower flickering faintly as if to remind her that some mysteries were best left undisturbed.

And from that night on, Lucy never walked past the old cemetery after dark again.

10

THE CREEPY ONES OF WANGARATTA

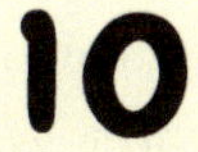

Stella and Derek had always dreamed of a fresh start. After years of city living, they decided to pack up and move to the country. They found a little farmhouse on a big block of land just outside Wangaratta, in rural Victoria. The house was small but charming, and it came with plenty of room for a garden, some chickens, and maybe even a few sheep. Surrounded by dense bushland, a winding creek, and no neighbours for miles, it seemed like the perfect place to build a new life.

"We're gonna love it here," Stella said, pulling into the long gravel driveway on their first day. "Just look at all the space, Derek! We can finally breathe."

Derek smiled, tossing their bags into the back of the house. "It's beautiful, love. Nice and quiet, just like we wanted. No more traffic, no more rush. Just us and the land."

The couple got to work unpacking and setting up their new home. As the sun set behind the hills, they sat out on the front porch, sipping cold beers, enjoying the peace and quiet. The only sounds were the distant calls of kookaburras and the rustling of the leaves in the trees.

"Couldn't ask for a better spot," Derek said, stretching his legs out on the wooden deck.

"I reckon," Stella agreed, her eyes scanning the bushland around them. The land felt wide, empty, and full of promise. "I'm looking forward to waking up with the birds singing every morning."

That night, after a hearty dinner, they settled into bed in their new farmhouse. The sounds of the country night were different from the city—quieter, softer—but there was something eerie about the stillness.

Stella stirred in bed. The wind had picked up, and the trees outside creaked and groaned. She glanced at the clock—it was nearly midnight. A strange feeling crept over her, like she was being watched.

"Everything okay, love?" Derek mumbled, half asleep.

"Yeah, just... feel a bit funny," Stella whispered, turning over. But she didn't mention it again. It was probably nothing—just the unfamiliar sounds of the country at night.

But as the hours passed, the feeling didn't go away. In fact, it only grew stronger. There were noises outside their window—soft whispers, footsteps. At first, Stella thought it was just the wind, or maybe a kangaroo hopping by. But then there was a *knock* on the window. A sharp, loud sound that sent a jolt through her.

"Did you hear that?" she whispered urgently to Derek.

Derek was awake now, eyes wide. "What the hell was that?"

Stella slowly pulled the curtain aside. Nothing. Just the dark, empty yard and the sway of the trees.

"Maybe a possum or something," Derek said, trying to reassure her.

But as they lay there, both tense and alert, a new noise came—a soft scrape against the side of the house. It wasn't an animal. It was too deliberate, too... human.

"Did you hear that?" Stella said again, her voice shaking now.

Derek nodded, sitting up. "Stay here. I'll go check it out."

He grabbed a flashlight from the bedside table, and Stella held her breath as Derek crept toward the front door. The sound of his boots on the old wooden floor was the only thing that broke the silence.

"Be careful," she whispered.

Derek nodded, then stepped outside, shining his light across the yard. For a long moment, he stood still, scanning the dark. The beam of the flashlight cut through the night, catching the reflection of something shiny in the distance. He frowned.

"Stella!" Derek called out. "Get in here, now!"

Stella rushed to the door.

"What is it?" she asked, her voice tight with fear.

Derek's face was pale, his hand trembling as he pointed toward the creek at the edge of their land. There, in the darkness, they saw figures moving—three or four people, standing just beyond the water's edge, hidden in the trees. They wore strange masks—white, featureless, with dark hollow eyes.

"Who are they?" Stella whispered, clinging to Derek.

"I don't know," Derek replied, voice tight with fear. "But they're not good news."

The figures in the masks stood still, watching them. A chilling silence hung in the air. Then, suddenly, they began to move toward the house.

"Quick!" Derek hissed, pulling Stella back inside. "Lock the door, now!"

They bolted the door and rushed to the windows, peeking out through the curtains. The masked figures were getting closer. Their movements were slow, deliberate, as if they knew exactly what they were doing.

"What do they want?" Stella whispered, her voice trembling.

"I don't know," Derek said, looking out the back window. "But they're heading for the house. We need to get out of here. They're not here to say 'G'day.'"

The sound of footsteps grew louder. The group had reached the front porch. There was another knock—this time at the front door, sharp and heavy. The masks were featureless, their eyes too dark to read. The people didn't speak—they just stood there, silent and still.

"Call the police," Stella urged, backing away from the window.

Derek fumbled for his phone, but there was no signal. The house was too far out, deep in the bush. They were alone.

"We need to hide," Derek said, his voice frantic. "There's nowhere to run!"

Just then, the door creaked. It wasn't locked. One of the figures was trying the handle.

The door groaned under the pressure. They couldn't hold it much longer.

"Upstairs!" Derek shouted. "Now!"

The two of them ran up the narrow staircase, hearts pounding in their chests. They could hear the sound of the door opening, the soft shuffle of feet across the floor below.

Stella grabbed Derek's arm, her face pale. "What do we do? We can't stay here!"

"We can't run," Derek said, his eyes darting around the room. "But we can make sure they don't find us."

They hid in the closet, holding their breath as the masked figures searched the house. The door to the closet creaked open, and for a moment, Stella's heart stopped. But it wasn't them. The searchers moved past, and the door closed again.

Outside, the night was quiet. No more footsteps. No more whispers. The figures were gone.

Stella and Derek stayed hidden until the first light of dawn broke through the windows. The house was still. Silent.

When they finally ventured outside, the yard was empty, and the masks were gone. But the feeling didn't leave.

They never saw the masked figures again, but every night, when the wind blew through the trees and the creek whispered, they could feel their eyes on them. And they always locked the doors—just in case.

About the Author

Heather Mallia is an Australian author with a passion for telling spooky tales that send shivers down your spine. With a background in education, Heather draws inspiration from the children she teaches, capturing their boundless curiosity and wonder to create eerie worlds filled with adventure and mystery.

When she's not writing, Heather can be found spending time with her beloved family, including her dog, Oliver, and her cat, Wednesday. A passionate creator, she enjoys drawing, painting, and gardening—finding joy in the quiet moments of creativity and the excitement of a well-told spooky story.

A lifelong fan of Halloween and all things eerie, Heather has always loved the chill that comes with a well-told ghost story. She wanted to put a distinctly Aussie twist on her tales, bringing her love for spooky stories to life in a way that reflects her home and experiences. Whether it's a haunted house in the bush or a ghostly figure lurking by the creek, Heather's stories offer a fresh, local take on the supernatural. Through her writing, Heather hopes to inspire young readers to embrace the thrill of adventure and explore the darker, mysterious corners of their imaginations.